All glory and praises to the most high YAH

REMEMBER
THE SABBATH
DAY AND KEEP IT HOLY
FOR IN SIX DAYS
THE LORD MADE
THE HEAVENS AND
THE EARTH
THE SEA
AND ALL
THAT IS
IN THEM
BUT HE
RESTED
ON THE
SEVENTH
DAY
EXODUS 20:8,11

Draw a line to match the parents to their babies.

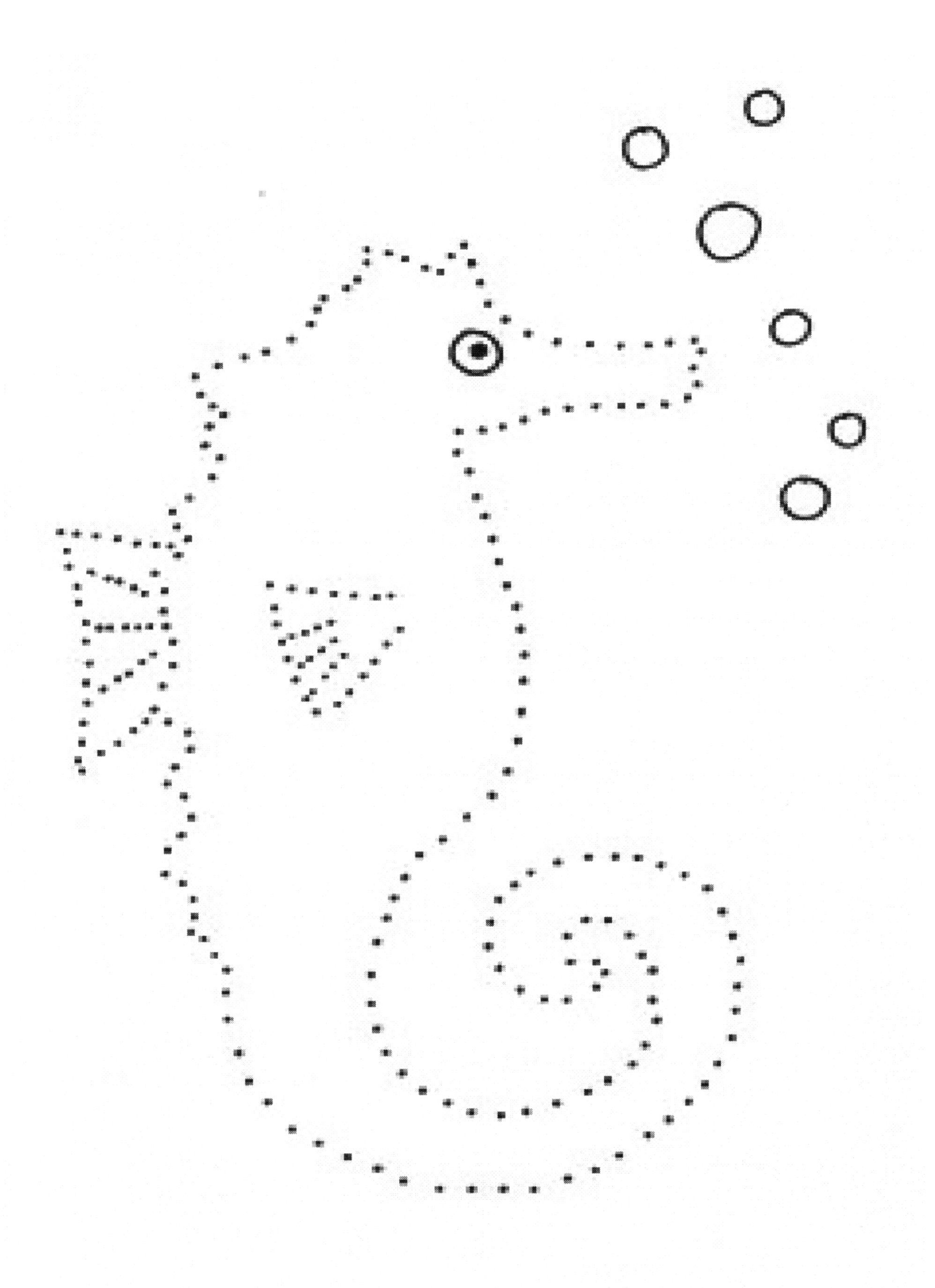

1. Light blue
2. Yellow
3. Pink
4. Brown
5. Orange
6. Dark blue
7. White
8. Green
9. Grey

drawing page

drawing page

drawing page

drawing page

drawing page

drawing page

drawing page

drawing page

drawing page

drawing page

drawing page

drawing page

drawing page

Printed in Great Britain
by Amazon